Frederick Lockwood Pierson

The Descendants of Stephen Pierson of Suffolk County,

England

Frederick Lockwood Pierson

The Descendants of Stephen Pierson of Suffolk County, England

ISBN/EAN: 9783744776691

Printed in Europe, USA, Canada, Australia, Japan

Cover: Foto ©Raphael Reischuk / pixelio.de

More available books at **www.hansebooks.com**

THE DESCENDANTS

OF

STEPHEN PIERSON

OF

SUFFOLK COUNTY, ENGLAND,

AND NEW HAVEN AND DERBY, CONN.

1645-1739.

———

By FREDERICK LOCKWOOD PIERSON,

Of Ellsworth, Litchfield Co., Conn.

———

AMENIA, N. Y.:
WALSH & GRIFFEN, PRINTERS.
1895.

PREFACE.

This book represents the work of over twenty-five years, in which the author has given all the time which could be spared from the cultivation of his farm in Ellsworth and his other business to the collection of its material. He has travelled over much of the states of Connecticut and New York to ascertain the facts and verify the statements he makes. It has been a long and tedious task, relieved however, by his affection and respect for his ancestry whose history he desired to perpetuate. He became early satisfied that the name borne by the family was Pierson and not Parsons, and he has adhered to that spelling throughout, notwithstanding the fact that many consider the latter correct. He regrets that many blanks still exist in the record. Much effort has been made to ascertain the name of the wife of Sergeant Abraham Pierson. As a last resort he inserted an enquiry in the genealogical column of the Mail and Express, but received only this answer; *"perhaps* she was a sister of George Beaumont of Derby and daughter of Thomas Beaumont of New Haven." He prefers "Sarah———" to that, as he believes the genealogist should deal only in facts. Bronson Olcott, who is desended from Hannah Chatfield, daughter of Sergeant Abraham, labored in vain to discover this name.

He desires to acknowledge assistance rendered him by Mr. E. N. Sheppard, who has furnished him part of his material.

F. L. P.

PIERSON GENEALOGY.

————o————

STEPHEN PIERSON, the Immigrant Ancestor, born in Suffolk County, England, in 1645, was apprenticed there by his mother (probably a widow) to Thomas Mulliner of Branford, Conn., to learn the carpenter trade, and landed in New Haven in 1654. Mulliner first appeared in New Haven in 1640.   June 30, 1657, Stephen testified in conrt in New Haven in a case of slander brought by Meeker against Mulliner for saying that Meeker's pigs were bewitched.   Oct., 1658, he appeared in the Probate Court at New Haven in a complaint made against Thomas Mulliner for not fulfilling an agreement to teach him the carpenter trade.   March 15, 1667, he was one of eight recorded residents of Derby, then called Paugassett, and in all probability was there in 1666.   His first wife, and mother of all his children, was Mary Tomlinson, daughter of Henry Tomlinson and his wife, Alice ——— of Stratford, Conn., who came from Watertown, Mass., in 1644; to Milford, Conn., in 1652 (where he kept an ordinary) ; and thence to Stratford, Conn., in 1665, where he died in 1681.   His widow, Alice, married John Birdsey, senior, under a contract of Oct. 8th, 1688.   Mary Tomlinson died in Derby Sept. 25, 1715.   Stephen died in Derby (now Oxford) May 14, 1739, aged 94, leaving a second wife, Esther.   He had a home lot of 3½ acres, now part of a town reservoir in Derby, on the original town street on meeting house hill, called also New Haven Sentinel hill.   His will, dated Sept. 2, 1733, provides for his wife, Esther; eldest son, Stephen, junior, 20 shillings; daughter, Sarah Twitchell, 80 pounds; daughter, Mary Baldwin, 80 pounds; son, Abraham, and daughter, Bathsheba Blackman, of Stratford, Conn., heretofore provided for ; (son, John, probably a bachelor, died about 1704).   His son, Abraham, appointed executor.   Inventory, dated Dec. 4, 1739, is as follows, viz. : Welchman's lot, £100; barn and homestead, £360; 80 acres of land in Quaker Farms purchase, £44; another piece of land in Bear Hill district, £85 ; one old Bible, 5 shillings ; one other Bible, 6 shillings ; and other small articles (requiring an expert to read) amounting in all to £631, 9s., 3d.   The appraisers were Francis French and Samuel Riggs.   All attempts to trace Stephen Pierson in Suffolk County or beyond have failed.

FIRST GENERATION.

Children of the Immigrant Stephen **Pierson** and Mary **Tomlinson**, all born in Derby. Conn. :

1.—*Sarah Pierson*, m. John Twitchell, Jan. 21, 1679.
2.—*Stephen Pierson, junior* (eldest son), m. Mehetabel Canfield, daughter of Thomas Canfield, Oct. 12, 1697.
3.—*Mary Pierson*, m. Josiah Baldwin Sept. 19, 1700.
4.—*John Pierson* (probably a bachelor), d. about 1704.
5.—*Bathsheba Pierson*, m. Adam Blackman of Stratford, Conn.
6.—*Abraham Pierson* (called Sergeant), b. in 1681; m. Sarah ——— (cannot learn her full name).
7.—*Daniel Pierson*, who drew lots in Oxford in 1713, was probably their son, but could find no proof of that fact.

SECOND GENERATION.

Children of 2 **Stephen Pierson, junior,** and **Mehetabel Canfield,** who was b. in Milford July 2, 1671 :

8.—*Elizabeth Pierson*, b. Jan. 12, 1699, in Derby; m. a Mr. Bennett.
9.—*Thomas Pierson*, b. in Derby; m. first Ruth Holbrook of Derby Feb. 22, 1727–8, in Norwalk; second widow Elizabeth Thomas of Norwalk March 7, 1738.
10.—*John Pierson*, b. in Derby in 1705; m. ——— Scrivener, daughter of Benjamin Scrivener of Norwalk; resided for a time in Norwalk, but d. in Huntington Jan. 25, 1789, aged 84. He had a son, William (whose wife was Hannah), and probably other children.
11.—*Job Pierson*, b. in Derby Oct. 5, 1707; d. in Derby in 1746–7, leaving a widow, Sarah, and sons, Stephen and Samuel.
12.—*Phebe Pierson*, b. in Derby; m. William Fanton.
13,—*Abigail Pierson*, b. in Derby; m. Mr. St. John.
14.—*Jonathan Pierson*, b. in Derby May 6, 1716; m. Mar. 5, 1739, Mary Bates.

Stephen Pierson, junior, died in Derby in 1744 intestate. Date of his wife's death has not been ascertained. His inventory list in 1717 was £51.

Children of **6 Sergeant Abraham Pierson, senior,** and **Sarah ——— :**

15.—*Sarah Pierson,* b. Aug. 19, 1705; m. Thomas Bassett Aug. 24, 1727, in Derby.

16.—*Abraham Pierson, junior,* b. July 26, 1707; m. April 10, 1731, Susannah Wooster, daughter of Sylvester Wooster, of Milford, and Susannah, his wife. Susannah Wooster, was born July 25, 1713.

17.—*Mary Pierson,* b. Oct. 26, 1712; m. John Sheppard, of Milford, in May, 1732; d. in Newtown in 1791. John Sheppard was b. Oct. 26, 1708, son of John Sheppard and Abigail Allen.

18.—*Hannah Pierson,* b. Aug. 4th, 1715; m. Solomon Chatfield June 12, 1734, in Derby.

19.—*Stephen Pierson, 3d,* b. March 4, 1720, in Derby; m. June 15, 1738, Hannah Munson, dau. of John and Elizabeth Munson, of Brookhaven, L. I. This family removed to New Albany.

20.—*Bathsheba Pierson,* b. Dec. 1, 1726. m. Ephraim Parker.

Abraham, senior, d. May 12, 1758. His will, dated April 26, 1750, is to be seen in New Haven. His list in 1717 was £48, 10s. He was Selectman in 1711.

THIRD GENERATION.

Children of 9 **Thomas** Pierson and Ruth **Holbrook,** daughter of Abil Holbrook, of Derby :

21.—*Mehetabel Pierson,* b. Jan. 13, 1729, in Norwalk, Ct.; m. Theophilus Hanton, of Norwalk, Ct.

22.—*Timothy Pierson,* b. in Norwalk Nov. 7, 1732; m. March 9, 1756, at Fairfield, Elizabeth Couch, dau. of Samuel Couch. (Simon Couch was the Immigrant Ancestor of the Couches.) She was b. June 13, 1735.

23.—*Nathan Pierson,* b. Nov. 27, 1734, in Norwalk; m. Nov. 17, 1756, Amy Smith.

24.—*Hannah Pierson,* b. in Norwalk ; m. Enos Bradley, of Derby, Nov. 7, 1751.

Ruth Holbrook, d. Oct. 14, 1737. Thomas Pierson m. second in Norwalk (and recorded there) wid. Elizabeth Thomas Mar-

7, 1738. He died in 1772 in Derby. No date of his second wife's death recorded.

Dec. 8, 1728, Thomas Pierson and Ruth, his wife, were among the list of persons who owned the half-way covenant during Rev. Mr. Stoddard's ministry in Woodbury. (See Cothren's History of Ancient Woodbury.)

Children of 14 **Jonathan Pierson** and **Mary Bates.**

25.—*Martha Pierson*, b. Jan. 12, 1740, d. young.

26.—*Elias Pierson*, b. June 23, 1743.

27.— *Osborn Pierson*, b. —— ; d. in Ohio (traditionary).

28.—*Bartholomew Pierson*, b. —— ; d. in Penn. (traditionary).

29.—*David Pierson*, b. —— ; d. in Sharon, Ct. (traditionary).

30.—*Jonathan Pierson, Jun.;* b. 1751 ; m. Elizabeth Thomas ; d. in Reading Sept. 7, 1818.

31.—*Martha Pierson, 2d ;* born March 4th, 1753.
   Nothing more is known of Martha and Elias.
   Mary Bates Pierson died in Derby Feb. 16, 1755, and Jonathan Pierson died in Ridgefield, Sullivan county, N. Y.

Children of 16 **Abraham Pierson, Jun.,** and Susannah **Wooster.**

32.— *Oliver Pierson*, b. March 25, 1732 ; m. Hannah Peet.

33.—*Stephen Pierson, 4th,* b. in 1738 ; d. in Newtown May 7, 1763, leaving a widow (Mary Camp ?) probably and dau. Sarah.

34.—*Elizabeth Pierson,* who m. Samuel Wooster.

35.—*Capt. David Pierson,* b. Jan. 17, 1748 ; m. Lois Thompson, Oct. 29, 1766. They settled in Amenia.

36.—*Abraham Pierson, 3d.* b. Feb. 11, 1746 ; m. Kesia Lines. of New Haven, July 2, 1767.

37.—*Avis Peirson,* b. Oct. 11, 1751.
   The Woosters were from Milford, Ct.
   Abraham Pierson, Junior, d. in 1781.

Children of 19 **Stephen Pierson, 3d, and Hannah Munson.**
She was b. March 7, 1721 ; dau. of John and Elizabeth Munson of
Derby and grand-daughter of John and Hannah Munson of Brook-
haven, L. I. In 1770 this Munson family had removed to New
Concord, Albany Co., N. Y. They are descendants of Thomas
Munson of New Haven, Conn.

38.—*Enoch Pierson,* b. June 18, 1739, in Derby ; m. Abigail
   Clogstone of Reading, Conn., Feb. 11, 1761, in Newtown.
   She was b. March 22, 1738, in Reading.

39.—*Elijah Pierson,* b. in Derby Dec. 26, 1740; d. young and unmarried.

40.—*Rachel Pierson,* b. in Derby Sept. 16, 1742 ; m. Henry Clinton. He d. in North Colebrook, Conn., April 15, 1814, in
   his 87th year. Rachel d. in North Colebrook June 26, 1815.
   They had a large family. Some of them emigrated to Newark
   Valley, Tioga Co., N. Y.

41.—*Daniel Pierson,* b. April 29, 1744; m. ———. Was a soldier
   in the Revolutionary war ; left his wife for misconduct in his
   absence and took *his* two children and went west to parts
   unknown.

42.—*Eli Pierson,* b. in Derby in 1750; m. Sarah Hinman of
   Derby.

Stephen Pierson, 3d, d. in Derby in 1754, and his wid. m. Elijah Davis, who survived him and d. in Alford, Berkshire Co., Mass.,
Nov. 19, 1815, leaving a large family. His will is dated Feb. 2,
1753. Jabez Davis was one of her sons, living in Alford. Hannah
was her dau. She m. 1st Lewis, 2d Cline, 3d Mitchel in Egremont,
North part.

FOURTH GENERATION.

Children of 22 **Timothy** Pierson and **Elizabeth** Couch,
who were m. March 9, 1756, at Fairfield, Conn.

43.—*Sabary Pierson,* b. Feb. 26, 1758 ; m. Frances **Andrews** and
   removed to Newark, N. J.; had sons and daughters.

44.—*Abigail Pierson,* b. April 20, 1760.

45.—*Daniel Pierson,* b. March 30, 1762. Settled in Tioga Co., N. Y.

46.—*Abraham Pierson,* b. Feb. 20, 1764; m. Urana Starr.

47.—*Samuel Pierson*, b. Dec. 15, 1765. Was a doctor and resided in Columbus, O., and had a son, George M. Pierson. His father died when he was very young. He became a lawyer and member of congress.

48.—*Elijah Pierson*, b. Feb. 6, 1768. He had two sons, Jared and Timothy, and one dau., Betsey, who m. Lemuel Adams of Reading, Conn. They had two sons, Lemuel and Stephen Adams. Timothy d. in Georgetown, Conn.

49.—*Betty Pierson*, b. Nov. 7, 1770.

50.—*Hannah Pierson*, b. Aug. 12, 1773.

51.—*Eleanor Pierson*, b. July 22, 1775.

52.—*Aaron Pierson*, b. Jan. 12, 1779.

Timothy Pierson d. in Reading, Conn., but resided for a time previously in Saugatuck, now Westport. His family opposed his marrying Miss Couch because she was poor. Many of this family spell their name *Parsons*.

Children of 23 **Nathan Pierson** and **Amy Smith**.

53.—*David Pierson*.

54.—*Thomas Pierson*.

55.—*Abel Pierson*, m. Hannah Fairchild.

56.—*Nathan Pierson, junior*. Some Nathan Pierson, m. Sarah Fairchild. They had a son, William, who d. Sept. 10, 1811, aged 9 months.

57.—*Ruth Pierson*.

58.—*Rebecca Pierson*.

59.—*Sarah Pierson*.

60.—*Hannah Pierson*.

Children of 30 **Jonathan Pierson, junior,** and **Elizabeth Thomas** of Norwalk, Conn.

61.—*Elias O. Pierson, 2d*, b. 1780; d. in Weston Sept. 29, 1851; m. Abigail ———.

62.—*Samuel G. Pierson*, b. 1785; d. in Reading Jan. 8, 1851; m. Hannah Hoyt.

63.—*Noah Pierson*, b. Jan. 30, 1795; d. Jan. 23, 1885, in Liberty, Sullivan Co., N. Y.; m. Jan. 27, 1822, Harriet Sanford, b. March 26, 1798. She d. in Liberty May 16, 1849. Noah Pierson and his wife went from Reading, Conn., to Liberty, N. Y., where they died. She had four or five brothers, among whom were Samuel of Reading, Conn., and George. The latter went south.

64.—*Sarah Pierson*, m. Turney Osborn of Norwalk, and had two sons, John, a teacher in Norwalk, and Gregory of Weston, Conn.

65.—*Phebe Pierson*, m. Alfred Rockwell of Marcellus, Onondago Co., N. Y.

Children of 32 Oliver Pierson and Hannah Peet.

66.—*Sarah Pierson*, bap. Sept. 20, 1750; m. ———— Baldwin.

67.—*Joseph Pierson* (eldest son), m. Sarah Sizer of Middletown, Conn.; d. in Cazenovia, N. Y.

68.—*Anna Pierson*, bap. July 25, 1756; m. ———— Hotchkiss.

69.—*Amos Pierson*, 2d, bap. Nov. 20, 1757; m. 1790, Sarah Johnson.

70.—*Huldah Pierson*, bap. June 3, 1759.

71.—*Susannah Pierson*, bap. May 9, 1762.

72.—*Hannah Pierson*, bap. May 26, 1765.

73.—*Isaac Pierson*, 3d, bap. April 12, 1767.

74.—*Lucy Pierson*, bap. August 21, 1768.

75.—*David Pierson*, bap. Nov. 25, 1770; m. March 6, 1791, Anna Botsford.

Children of 35 Capt. David Pierson and Lois Thompson.

(They generally spelled their name Parsons.)

76.—*Sarah Pierson*, b. Oct. 28, 1767; m. Samuel Falkner.

77.—*Joel Pierson*, m. Phebe Baylos.

78.—*Thompson Pierson*, m. Sally Welch. Settled in Chenango Co., N. Y.

79.—*David Pierson*, d. at the Forks, N. Y., 12 miles from Binghamton.

80.—*Truman Pierson*, m. Sally Barlo. He d. in Cairo, N. Y.

81.—*Joseph Pierson*, m. Polly Darling. He d. at Amenia, N. Y.,
    March 12, 1812, aged 34.   She d. May 27, 1851, aged 67.
82. —*Henrietta Pierson*, m. John Bayles of Catskill.
83.—*Lois Pierson*, m. Samuel Hood of Amenia.
84.—*Betsey Pierson*, m. Leman Bosworth and moved to Ohio.
85·—*Apame Pierson*, m. John Palmer of Poughkeepsie.

Capt. David Pierson d. in Amenia March 12, 1812, in his 64th
year.   Lois Thompson Pierson d. March 7, 1812, in her 62d year.
She was dau. of Capt. Jabez Thompson (a sea captain) and his
wife Sarah ———· of Derby.   Capt. Thompson was at one time
wealthy, but lost his money.   He resided about half way between
Birmingham and Ansonia on the upper side of the road.

Children of 36 **Abraham Pierson, 3d**, and **Keziah Lines**.

86.—*Susannah Pierson*, b. March 10, 1768; m. May 17, 1790,
    Lewis Loveland.
87.—*Abraham Pierson*, b. and d. same day.
88.—*Abraham Pierson, 4th*, bap. July 29, 1781.
89.—*Lines Pierson*, bap. May 23, 1773; d. in 1832 in Woodbridge.
    His children were Abraham, 5th, Jeremiah, Merritt, Lois and
    Harriet, who m. a Baldwin of Woodbridge.
90.—*Levi Pierson*, b. March 25, 1771 ; m. Emily ——— and lived
    in Orange.
91.—*Harriet Pierson*, m. 2 E. Russell; resided in Orange, Conn.,
    and had a large family.
92.—*Mary Pierson*.
93.—*Patty Pierson*.
94.—*Hannah Pierson*.
95.—*Amos Pierson*.

Abraham Pierson, 3d, d. in 1779–80, and had at his decease
the following living children : Levi, Lines, Mary, Patty, Hannah
and Amos, as appears by the records of the probate court.   Keziah
(Lines) Pierson d. in Woodbridge May 16, 1803.

Children of 38 **Enoch** Pierson and **Abigail Clogstone.**

96.—*Betsey Pierson,* b. in Newtown, March 17, 1762 ; m. ——— ;
d. May 14, 1829 ; m. Dea. Calvin Peck of Greenwich.   He d.
Sept. 1, 1847.

97.—*Mary Wakeman Pierson,* b. in Newtown Nov. 5, 1763 ; m.
David Tryon of Nine Partners, N. Y., and removed to Middle-
berg, Schoharie Co., N. Y. (New Connecticut).

98.—*Abigail Pierson,* b. in Ellsworth Jan. 5, 1766 ; m. Joel Hoyt
of Stanwich, Conn.

99.—*Amirillis Pierson,* b. in Ellsworth Sept. 2, 1768 ; m. John
Wells of Amenia, N. Y., and settled in Amsterdam, N. Y.

100.—*Stephen Pierson,* b. August 21, 1771, in Ellsworth ; m. Nov.
14, 1790, Hannah Curtis of Danbury.   He d. Dec. 9, 1839,
(suicide with opium).   She d. Feb. 3, 1844.

101.—*Enoch Pierson, junior,* b. May 9, 1773, in Ellsworth ; m. Feb.
8, 1795, Amy Studley of Ellsworth.   He d. Sept. 10, 1835.
She d. Feb. 9, 1846.

102.—*Freeman Washington Pierson,* b. March 16, 1776 ; in Ellsworth at the homestead ; m. Mary Skiff of Ellsworth October,
1797.   She was b. Sept. 23, 1774, in Ellsworth.

103.—*Amideus Pierson,* b. April 29, 1780, in Ellsworth ; m. Aurelia
Miles, Watertown, Conn., Feb. 7, 1808.   She was b. July 10,
1784.

Abigail Clogstone d. June 6, 1807, and Enoch m. 2d Abigail
Royce (maiden name), wid. of Dea. Silas St. John Oct. 8, 1809.
She d. Nov. 12, 1823.   Enoch d. Oct. 1, 1827.   Capt. Enoch, after
the death of his father (being too young to enlist), went as a servant
of an officer to Canada in the French war of 1755 ; returned,
learned the carpenter's trade, worked in Newtown till he removed to
Ellsworth April 9, 1764, and occasionally afterwards.   He was
appointed to line the Psalms in the Congregational Church of
Ellsworth, was selectman and constable and represented Sharon in
the General Assembly in October, 1795.   The homestead he first
purchased of John Jackson of 14 acres contained a house, barn and
orchard.   Capt. Enoch was five feet ten high, weight 180 pounds,
slightly Roman nose, gray eyes and brown hair.   Abigail, his first
wife, was tall and bony, black eyes and hair and Roman nose.

Children of 40 **Rachel Pierson** and **Henry Clinton.**

104.—*Henry Clinton*, d. in Wisconsin.

105.—*Sheldon Clinton*, d. in Wisconsin.

106.—*Samuel Clinton*, d. in Pennsylvania.

107.—*Lyman Clinton*, *1st*, d. in Newark Valley, Tioga county, N.Y.

108.—*Clara* or *Clarana*, wife of Ira Andrus of Colebrook, Conn.,
d. there ; left a large family.

109.—*Elijah Pierson Clinton*, bapt. April 18, 1762.

Henry Clinton died in Colebrook, Conn., April 15, 1814, in
his 87th year. He was a farmer and resided a while in New
Milford, Conn.   Rachel, his wife, died in Colebrook, Conn., June
26, 1815 ; born in Derby Sept. 16, 1742.

Children of 42 **Eli Pierson, Sr.,** and **Sarah Hinman.**

110.—*Betsey Pierson.*

111.—*Lewis Pierson.* b. 1772 in Derby ; m. Esther Smith of Derby.

112.—*Sarah Pierson.*

113.—*Lucy Pierson.*   A fine looking, intelligent young lady ; was
thrown from a wagon and crippled for life ; had no use of her
lower limbs, and occupied a swing bed the remainder of her
days, which were not a few.

All born in Derby (no dates).   All died in South Egremont,
Mass.   The daughters never married.   Eli Pierson died in Egremont May 22, 1822, aged 72 years.   Occupation, farming.   Sarah
Hinman Pierson died in South Egremont, Mass., March 9, 1815,
in her 68th year.

FIFTH GENERATION.

Children of 45 **Daniel Pierson.**

114.—*Samuel Pierson, M. D.*, settled in Columbus, Ohio.

115.—*Uriah Pierson.*

116.—*Betty Pierson.*

117.—*Clara Pierson.*

118.—*Hannah Pierson.*

119.—*Eunice Pierson.*

120.—*Lydia Pierson.*

121.—*Mary Pierson.*

122.—*Daniel Pierson.*

123.—*Burr Pierson.*

Children of 46 **Abraham Pierson** and **Urana Starr.**

124.—*Starr Pierson* b. Feb. 15, 1793 ; d. in Newark, N. J., Jan. 25.
1867 ; m. Elizabeth Spear of Bloomfield, N. J., Oct. 15. 1814
She was b. April 6, 1792 ; d. April 1. 1869.

125.—*Betsey Pierson* m. Rufus H. Pickett of Ridgefield, Conn.

126.—*Laura Pierson* m. Moses S. Betts of Fairfield, Conn.

Children of 55 **Abel Pierson** and **Hannah Fairchild.**

127.—*Nathan Pierson* m. Sally Swift (some Nathan d. in Derby.
Conn., Oct. 17, 1822, aged 40).

128.—*Hannah Pierson.*

129.—*Abial Pierson* m Dec. 25, 1806, Irene Holbrook and removed to Burton, New Connecticut, Ohio.

130.—*Abel Pierson* m. Merib Lyman and settled in Newark, N. J.
They had children and grandchildren.

131.—*Sheldon Pierson* b. in Derby 1791 ; m. Hepsey Peat.

132.—*Sophia Pierson* m. Bennet Hine of Naugatuck and d. leaving one son who has since died.

Children of 61 **Elias O. Pierson** and **Abigail Fanton.**

133.—*Charles Meeker Pierson* b. in Reading, Conn., June 1, 1815;
d. in Weston, Aug. 2, 1888, and buried at Easton.   He m.
Huldah M. Somers and had one child only, David Somers
Pierson, who was b. Oct. 18, 1842.

Children of 62 **Samuel C. Pierson** and **Hannah Hoyt.**

134.—*Daniel Pierson*, who d. in Norwalk, Conn., 1875.
135.—*Andrew Pierson*, who resides in Norwalk.

Children of 63 **Noah Pierson** and **Harriet Sanford.**

136.—*Ebenezer S. Pierson* b. Sept. 20, 1822 ;   m. May 23, 1849.
Harriet Griswold.   A son, Thomas, lives at Walton, Delaware
Co., N. Y., and another son, F. L. Pierson, is an engineer in a
steam saw-mill in the same county (?).
137.—*Mary E. Pierson* b. April 21, 1824;   m. Eri Chamberlain
Nov. 23, 1848.
138.—*John T. Pierson*, b. Oct. 28, 1825 ; m. Martha Young, Nov.
26, 1850.
139.—*Samuel G. Pierson*, b. May 17, 1827 ; drowned Oct. 12, 1846.
140.—*Sarah C. Pierson* b. April 4, 1829; d. March 3, 1830.
141.—*Sarah C. Pierson*, 2d, b. Dec. 11, 1830 ; m. James W. Smith
May 14, 1860.   Smith resides in Iowa.
142.—*Noah B. Pierson* b. Jan. 14, 1833 ; killed at Cedar Mountain Sept. 19, 1862.
143.—*Esther C. Pierson* b. Sept. 22, 1835 ; m. John Brundage,
Nov. 23, 1854.   She died Sept. 6, 1869.
144.—*Alfred R. Pierson* b. Aug. 31, 1837 ; killed at the battle of
Cedar Mountain Aug. 9, 1862.
145.—*Le Grand Pierson* b. Jan. 17, 1840; d. May 11, 1840.
146.—*Hannah E. Pierson* b. April 8, 1841 ; m. John F. Burch
March 5, 1859, and d. Feb. 12, 1865.
147.—*Harriet A. Pierson* b. March 9, 1843 ; m. Arthur McKinney
Dec. 3, 1873.

Children of 67 **Joseph Pierson** and **Sarah Sizer.**

148.— *Oliver Pierson* settled in Monticello, N. Y.

149.— *Abel Pierson* lived with his father in Cazenovia, N. Y.

150.— *William Pierson* b. May 18, 1775; m. Betsey Sawyer of Cornwall, Conn.; d. in Illyria, O. A story is told of his having bitten a rattlesnake with his teeth. His wife died in Cornwall, Conn.

151.— *Sarah Pierson* bap. April 28, 1782.

152.— *Martin Pierson.*

153.— *Reuben Pierson.*

154.— *Josiah Pierson.*

155.— *Isaac Pierson.*

156.— *David Pierson.*

157.— *Polly Pierson.*

158.— *Ichabod Spencer Pierson,* a lawyer of Utica, N. Y.

159.— *Ruby Pierson.*

160.— *Lucy Pierson.*

Children of 77 **Joel Pierson** and **Phebe Bayles.**

161.— *Orrin Pierson* m. Betsey Prosier.

162.— *Austin Pierson.*

163 — *Jabez Pierson.*

164.— *Milton Pierson.*

165.— *Eli Pierson.*

166.— *Laura Pierson.*

167.— *Phebe Pierson.*

168.— *Anna Pierson.*

169.— *Paulina Pierson* d. at the manor unm.

170.— *George Pierson,* resided in Wayne Co., Pa.

Children of 80 **Truman** Pierson and **Sally Barlo.**

171.— *Electa Pierson* m. ——— Richmond of Cairo, Greene Co., N. Y.

172.— *Barlow Pierson* m. ——— Barker of Catskill, N. Y.

173.— *Sanford Pierson.*

174.—*Sarah Pierson* m. ——— Bevins.

175.—*Eunice Boyd Pierson* m. William H. Hayes.

176.—*Joel Pierson* rem. to Ohio.

177.—*Philo Pierson* rem. to Ohio.

178.—*Clark Pierson* rem. to Ohio.

179.—*Harriet Pierson* m. ——— Lockwood of N. Y. city.

Children of 81 **Joseph Pierson** and **Polly Darling.**

180.—*Parnel Pierson* b. Feb. 13, 1802 ; m. Henry Bird ; has son, Milo.

181.—*Julia Pierson* b. Feb. 20, 1804 ; m. Augustus Jarvis.

182.—*Warren Pierson* b 1805 ; m. Caroline Rowe. He was killed Aug. 1, 1872, by a two-year-old bull in Amenia. His wife d. of cancer June 5. 1885, aged 71.

183.—*Almira Pierson* b. Nov. 11. 1809 ; d. April 16, ——— ; m. Milton Andrews.

184.—*Mary Allen Pierson* b. Nov. 11, 1812 ; m. George Delevan ; d. Oct. 7, 1876.

Children of 96 **Betsey Pierson** and **Calvin Peck** of Greenwich.

185.—*Polly Peck* b. Aug. 18, 1785, in Greenwich ; m. Luther Chaffee of Ellsworth. She died in Ellsworth April 5, 1866.

186.—*Enoch Pierson Peck* b. in Greenwich Nov. 14, 1787 ; m. Mary Peck of Greenwich He died Aug. 24. 1858, in Sharon.

187.—*George Whitfield Peck* b. in Ellsworth Dec. 5, 1789 ; m. 1st Hannah Lockwood of Watertown, Conn. ; 2d Charlotte Peck of Greenwich. He died in Greenwich Jan. 25, 1870.

188.—*Sarah Peck* b. Oct. 7, 1791, in Ellsworth ; m. Lewis Peck of Greenwich. She died Sept. 10, 1871, in Ellsworth.

189.—*Amirillis Peck* b. Dec. 10, 1794 ; d. Nov. 8, 1828, unm.

190.—*Betsey Peck* b. Jan. 29, 1797 ; m. John Wells, Jun., of Amsterdam, N. Y. She died in Amsterdam.

191.—*Laura Peck* b. Dec. 19, 1798 ; m. John Hennings of New York. She died Aug. 29, 1871, in Ellsworth, a widow.

192.—*John Calvin Peck* b. Oct. 14, 1800; m. Sarah VanLoan of Athens, N. Y. He died Dec. 17, 1846.

193.—*Samuel Ferris Peck* b. Dec. 7, 1802; m. Laura Ann Pierson. He died Sept. 3, 1864. This family is extinct. Laura Ann Pierson died Dec. 25, 1880. Her daughter, Charlotte, and grand-daughter, Charlotte, both died before her.

Children of 97 **Mary Wakeman Pierson** and **David Tryon** of Nine Partners, N. Y.

194.—*Betsey Tryon* m. 1st George Brownell, 2d Lyman Seeley.

195.—*Amelia Tryon* m. Judson Tyrrel and removed to Fowler, Trumbull Co., Ohio.

196.—*Aurelia Tryon* m. Lewis Evans and removed to Michigan.

197.—*Oliver Tryon* m. Huldah Benedict of Schoharie Co., N. Y.

198.—*Alma Tryon* m. Headley Spencer of Schoharie Co., N. Y.

199.—*Phebe Tryon* m. Amos Sanford of Schoharie Co., N. Y.

200.—*Freeman Tryon* m. Phebe Tallman.

201.—*Eunice Tryon* m. Peter Shaver.

202.—*Harriet Tryon* m. 1st Headley Spencer, 2d James Borden, and removed to Illinois.

203.—*David Tryon* m. Mary Benedict.

204.—*Stephen Tryon* m. Effa Hilts.

205.—*Enoch Tryon* m. Percy Maker, and 6 more died too young to name.

Mary Wakeman Pierson was named after the Wakemans of Fairfield, Conn.; her mother was Abigail Clogstone. Nicholas Clogstone married Mary Wakeman of Fairfield, a near relative of Rev. —— Wakeman of Fairfield

Children of 98 **Abigail** Pierson and **Joel Hoyt.**

206.—*Mehetabel Hoyt* b. June 16, 1791; d. Jan. 29th, 1810, unm.

207.—*Freeman Hoyt* b. Jan. 16, 1795; d. in Stanwich March 16, 1869, aged 74 years and 2 months; m. Lorina Finch. No children. She died in Stanwich Mar. 21, 1861, aged 81.

Joel Hoyt was drowned in the river June 6, 1805, aged 49 years 2 months and 20 days. Abigail, his wife, d. in Stanwich Aug. 1, 1848, in her 84th year. This Hoyt family were buried in their family burying ground on their farm in Stanwich and are extinct.

Children of 99 **Amirillis Pierson** and **John Wells.**

208.—*Abigail Wells.*
209.—*Anna Wells.*
210.—*Julia Wells.*
211.—*John Wells, Jun.*
213.—*Almena Wells.*
214.—*Pierson Wells* d. when 15 years old in Amsterdam, N. Y.

All the above children were born in Nobletown, N. Y., but the family moved to Amsterdam where both parents died. John Wells bought a farm and paid for it ; got a bad title and lost it. Then he bought it of the rightful owner and paid for it again.

Children of 100 **Stephen Pierson** and **Hannah Curtis.**

215.—*Ada Pierson* b. June 16, 1792 ; d. Jan. 9, 1813, unm.
216.—*Abigail Pierson* b. April 28, 1794 ; m. Lewis Burr Sturges (his 2d wife), and died without issue. (His 1st wife was —— Abels, 3d Wid. McMurtry.)
217.—*Zilla Pierson*, b. April 5, 1796 ; m. Clark Sherwood. She died Sept. 2, 1843, aged 47 years and 5 months.
218.—*Miritta Pierson* b. Jan. 5, 1798 ; d. Jan. 14, 1813, unm.
219.—*Stephen Curtis Pierson* b. Nov. 19, 1799 ; d. Feb. 13, 1869 ; m. Sabra Heath, Nov. 19, 1822, in Sharon. She was born April 6, 1798.
220.—*Betsey Maria Pierson* b. Oct. 9, 1801 ; m. 1st Joseph Heath, 2d Alexander Conn.
221.—*Lucy Pierson* b. March 26, 1805 ; d. July 2, 1805.
222.—*Lucy Lovina Pierson* b. March 31, 1807 ; d. Nov. 16, 1809.
223.—*Heman King Pierson* b. Dec. 22, 1808 ; m. Janette Upson of Watertown, Conn. She died Jan. 27, 1884, in Tallmadge, Ohio. He died Oct. 31, 1890, in Ashtabula, Ohio, of softening of the brain. Both buried in Tallmadge.

224.—*Noah Seth Pierson* b. Feb. 26, 1811; m. 1st Susan Lattison; 2d, Feb. 21, 1864, Mary E. Fuller, who was b. Aug. 9, 1845, in Unadilla, Otsego Co., N. Y. He died in Unadilla May 1, 1875, and the widow married again.

Children of 101 **Enoch** Pierson, Jun., and **Amy Studley.**

225.—*Polly Pierson*, m. Philander Hatch of New Preston ; d. without children.

226.—*Ruth Pierson*, d. unm.

227.—*Amy Pierson*, twin with Ruth, m. Burr Camp of New Preston, Conn.

228.—*Mary Ann Pierson*, d. March 6, 1846, unm.

229.— *Caroline Pierson*, m. Dr. Russel Everett and d. April 13, 1852. She had two sons (*a*) Enoch Pierson Everett, who m. 1st Helen Sophronia Everett, dau. of Dea. Wm. Everett and Sarah Gordon. They had two children, Frank Everett and William Everett. Enoch P. Everett m. 2d Emily Goodenough and has three children, Helen, Alice and Florence Everett. (*b*) Richard Floyd Everett, who m. Catharine St. John, dau. of Henry St. John and ———— Wheeler, his first wife.

101 Enoch Pierson, Jun., had no sons. He had blue eyes, dark hair, was six feet high and weighed over two hundred pounds.

Children of 102 **Freeman Washington Pierson** and **Mary Skiff.**

230.—*John Pierson*, b. Nov. 6, 1799, in Ellsworth, at the old homestead ; m. Sarah Lockwood of Greenwich, Conn., Nov. 30, 1821. She was b. Sept. 19, 1799, in Greenwich.

231.—*Betsey Pierson*, b. Jan. 17, 1802, at the old homestead ; m. 1st Edmund Miles Bennett of Sharon, Oct. 4, 1818; he was b. Nov. 22, 1796, in Sharon and was killed blasting in a well in Ellsworth Sept. 10, 1830. 2d Charles Lockwood of Greenwich April 3, 1842 ; he was b. April 13, 1797, and d. in Greenwich Sept. 28, 1852. Betsey d. in Sharon March 26, 1885 ; buried in Ellsworth ; no children.

232.—*Daniel Pierson*, b. Sept. 14. 1804, in Ellsworth ; m. Electa
Ann Reed of Sharon Sept. 15, 1828, b. Feb. 18, 1808.

233.—*Paulina Pierson*, b. March 15, 1806 ; m. Ethan Lord of Ellsworth Nov. 20, 1827.

234.—*Mary Louisa Pierson*, b. Dec. 11, 1812 ; m. Augustus L.
Peck of Ellsworth Jan. 6, 1841. He died Jan. 22, 1883, of
dropsy. She died Sept. 6, 1888 ; buried in Ellsworth ; no
children.

Mary Skiff died Nov. 18, 1846, and Freeman Washington
Pierson married 2d Miss Maria Boardman, who survived him and
died in Bridgewater. He died July 21, 1861, of a shock of palsy ;
never spoke again. He was five feet ten high, weighed 196, eyes
black, hair dark, which he lost by fever and became bald. His
breast measure was 42 inches in his old age and after he had lost
his flesh. Mary Skiff, mother of all his children, was about five
feet four high, weighed 200, blue eyes and dark brown hair. He
was a well read, intellectual man and often selectman and constable.

Children of 103 **Amideus Pierson** and **Aurelia Miles.**

235.—*Laura Ann Pierson*, b. July 29, 1810 ; m. Samuel F. Peck
(her cousin). She d. Dec. 25, 1880. Her husband, dau. Charlotte and grand-daughter Charlotte died before her.

236.—*Charles Miles Pierson*, b. March 13, 1812 ; d. unm. in Norfolk, Conn., Aug. 2, 1872 ; buried in Ellsworth.

237.—*Almira Pierson*. b. March 6, 1815. She was 2d wife of Henry
St. John, son of Silas St. John and Olive Barstow.

238.—*Aurelia Pierson*, m. Wm. E. Marsh.

239.—*Pluma B. Pierson*, m. Horace Stannard of Norfolk, Conn.

240.—*Cordelia Pierson*, d. unm.

241.—*Isabel Pierson*, m. Ebenezer M. Johnson of Cornwall.

Amideus Pierson died July 31, 1866. His wife died. Jan. 13,
1871, aged 86 years, 6 months and 3 days. Both buried in Ells·
worth. She was dau. of Richard Miles and Margaret Scott. The
Miles are descended from Richard Miles, who landed in Boston
and removed thence to New Haven, Conn. Isabella has two children, daughter Olive and son Harry. Pluma has no children, nor
Aurelia M.

Children of 111 **Lewis** Pierson and **Esther Smith** of Derby (spelling the name Parsons).

242.—*Elijah Pierson*, b. in 1798; d. unm. in South Egremont, Mass., April 5, 1861 (suicide); wagon maker.

243.—*Eli Pierson, Jun.*(blacksmith), b.in 1799; m. Clarissa Tuller.

244.—*Maria Pierson*, d. of palsy unm. in Egremont.

245.—*Esther Pierson*, m. Charles Beers and had four children, viz: Eliza Ann, Maria, Frank and Fanny. This family reside in the state of New York—Marcellus, Onondago county.

246.—*Anna Pierson*, b. in 1806; d. Aug. 30, 1833, unm.

247.—*Lewis Smith Pierson*, b. in Egremont; m. Elizabeth Boardman of Sheffield, Mass.

248.—*Sarah Pierson*, 2d wife of David Stillman of Sheffield; had a dau. d. young and unm. and a son Charles, who m. Del. Curtis of Sheffield and removed after the death of his parents to California. He has a daughter. David and Sarah Stillman were both murdered by a mulatto in their home at Sheffield Nov. 29, 1877, Thanksgiving evening, for which he was hung.

Lewis Pierson died in Egremont May 10, 1859. Esther Smith (his wife) died Oct. 4, 1829, aged 54. She was a daughter of Elijah Smith of Oxford. Her son, Eli, learned the blacksmith trade of her brother, Isaac Smith of Oxford.

SIXTH GENERATION.

Children of 124 **Starr** Pierson and **Elizabeth Spear.**

250.—*Caroline Pierson*, b. March 12, 1816; 2d wife (prob.) of Moses G. Betts.

251.—*William Pierson*, b. Dec. 20, 1817.

252.—*Charles Pierson*, b. March 6, 1820; resides in Newark, N. J.

253.—*Walter Pierson*, b. Dec. 25, 1822; resides in Newark, N. J.

254.—*Laura Pierson*. b. April 13, 1824; resides in Bloomfield, N. J.

255.—*Rev. Benjamin Pierson*, b. Jan. 6. 1826; did live in Michigan.

256.—*Cyrus Pierson*, b. March 18, 1828; lives in Bloomfield.

257.—*Abraham Pierson*, b. Aug. 3, 1830; resides in Newark.

258.—*Henry Clay Pierson* b. May 12, 1833; resides in Newark.

Children of 127 **Nathan Pierson** and **Sally Swift.**

259.—*John Swift Pierson*, d. in Brooklyn, N. Y., June 21, 1874; m. Eliza Jennings of Fairfield, Conn., who d. young, leaving a son, John Augustus Pierson.

260.—*Abel Pierson*, d. unm.

261.—*Edward Pierson*, m. Sarah Bennett and had one dau., Sarah Medora Bennett, who d. July, 1879, unm.

262.—*Abigail Pierson*, d. unm.

263.—*Martha B. Pierson*, m. Augustus Studwell.

Children of 131 **Sheldon Pierson** and **Hepsey Post.**

264.—*William R. Pierson* of Nichols Farms, m. Oct. 4. 1846. Augusta Wheeler. Had children, 1 Mary Augusta Pierson (who m. Sept. 26, 1866, Lorenzo B. Nichols, who d. Oct. 5. 1876); 2 America Pierson. and 3 Sarah Medora Pierson.

265.—*Sheldon P. Pierson. Jr.*, m. Lydia J. Hawley; no children. He lived in Trumbull.

Children of 150 **William** Pierson and **Betsey Sawyer.**

266.—*Polly Pierson*. b. Feb. 28, 1801; m. John Slade and had two children, Merritt Slade, who m. Sarah Wedge and resides in Cornwall, and Michael Slade.

267.—*Paulina Pierson*, b. Nov. 19, 1803 ; m. Roswell Perry.   She died in Winsted, Conn.

268.—*Maria Pierson*, b. Feb. 16, 1807.

269.—*Cornelia Pierson*, b. Sep. 29, 1809 ; m. Joseph Driggs.   She died in Michigan.

270.—*Ruby Pierson.*, b. March 5, 1813.

271.—*Clark Pierson*, b. March 12. 1817.   m.

272.—*Oliver Pierson*, b. Oct. 29, 1821.   He resided in Ohio and had a son, William H. Pierson and a daughter, Adelia, who m. ——— Gardiner and resides in Kansas.

Children of 161 **Orrin Pierson** and **Betsey Prosier.**

273.—*Austin Pierson*, m. Betsey Weaver.

274.—*Jabez Pierson*, m. Catharine Prosier.

275.—*Milton Pierson.* m. Eliza ——— .

276.—*Eli Pierson*, died in Hudson unm.

277.—*Laura Pierson*, m. 1st Joel Westfall and had two sons ; m. 2d Abiah Palmer and had one son, Abiah Palmer.

278.—*Phebe Pierson*, resides in Hudson, unm.

279 —*Anna Pierson*, m. and soon died.   Left no heirs.

NOTE.—Laura Pierson Palmer's son, Abiah W. Palmer, was president of the bank ; m. Miss Yeomans of Westfield, Mass. He died and she m. again. Laura Pierson Palmer was shot at through a window in the evening—just before Abiah, Jr., was born. The object was to destroy the heir prospective. The charge of shot just grazed the top of her head and failed of its purpose. It frightened her but did not seriously injure her or heir. The would be murderer (a man named Palmer) was arrested and convicted.

Children of 182 **Warren Pierson (or Parsons)** and **Caroline Rowe.**

280.—*Theron W. Pierson*, b. April 9, 1838 ; m. Feb. 28, 1861, Mary C. Burton, who was b. June 27, 1840, and resides (1887) in Washington, D. C. They have two children, Warren, b. Jan. 2, 1862, and Harry, b. Feb. 16, 1871.

281.—*Charles A. Pierson*, m. Oct. 6, 1874, Julia Smith ; b. Dec. 27, 1842 ; resided in 1884 in Amenia. They have two children, Carrie. b. Mar. 26, 1877, and George. b. Sept. 5, 1880.

282.—*Frank Pierson*, b. May 28, 1851 ; d in Amenia May 17, 1881.

283.—*Frances Pierson*, b. May 28, 1851 (twin with Frank).

Children of 217 Zillah Pierson and Clark Sherwood.

284.—*Stephen Pierson Sherwood*, b. Jan. 28, 1814.

285.—*Mary Sherwood*, b. July 26, 1817 ; d. April 5, 1823.

286.—*Henry Sherwood*, b. Mar. 24, 1819 ; d. May 27, 1820.

287.—*Seth Curtis Sherwood*, b. Sept. 10, 1821 ; d. Dec. 24, 1857.

288.—*Lois Ann Sherwood*, b. July 19, 1827.

Clark Sherwood died Feb. 19, 1854, aged 65 years.

Stephen P. Sherwood and Mary Hitchcock were married July 13, 1834. She died Feb. 6, 1855. Wm. Henry Sherwood, their son, was born April 13, 1835, and died March 28, 1852. Merritt E. Sherwood was born June 30, 1840, and resides in 1891 in New Milford. Stephen P. Sherwood and Jerusha Stark were married Oct. 10, 1855. She died Sept. 16, 1872, aged 54. Mary Eliza Sherwood was born Jan. 10, 1857, and was the wife of Charles Townsend of Pawling, N. Y. Frederick Sherwood was born Jan. 9, 1860, and died July 16, 1869.

Children of 219 Stephen Curtis Pierson and Sabra Heath.

289.—*Henry Clark Pierson*, b. June 6, 1823, in Ellsworth.

290.—*Marilla Cecilia Pierson*, b. July 13, 1826, in Ellsworth ; m. May 18, 1847, Alonzo Kingsley of New Preston, who was b. Oct. 3, 1828.

292.—*Milo Curtis Pierson*, b. July 13, 1828.   He m. Mary Maria Elmore Feb. 20, 1866, an Irish girl of Albany ; no children. He committed suicide by stabbing himself in the heart—a bad case of heart disease—June 24, 1890, aged 61 yrs., 11 mos., and 11 days.

293.—*Amelia Jane Pierson*, b. Aug. 6, 1833, in Ellsworth ; m. Aug. 1, 1856, in Patterson, N. Y., James Harvey Moore.   She died

in New Preston of pneumonia Jan. 8, 1885.   Jas. H. Moore
was born in Sharon Jan. 30, 1833.   Their children were Robert Moore, who m. ——— ; John, who m. ——— ; and Es-
telle, who m. ——— Warner, a blacksmith of New Preston.

294.—*Charles Elmore Pierson*, b. April 15, 1835 ; d. young in
Eugene, Ind.

295.—*Stephen Curtis Pierson*, b. August 26, 1838 ; d. young in
Eugene, Ind.

Sabra Heath Pierson (who was dau. of Obadiah Heath and
Diana Waller) d. in Eugene, Vermillion Co., Indiana, Sept. 4, 1838,
Stephen Curtis Pierson m. 2d Sarah Cooper, who was b. in Ellsworth
and d. there Aug. 14, 1888, aged 82 yrs.

Children of 223 **Heman King Pierson** and **Janette Upson.**

296.—*Fredrick Pierson*, d. young and unm.

297.—*Almira Pierson*, d. young and unm.

298.—*Elizabeth Pierson*, b. Sept. 11, 1837 ; m. Sept. 6, 1857, James
H. Bailey, who was b. Oct. 9, 1835.   She died in North East,
Mass.

Children of 224 **Noah Seth Pierson** and **Susan Lattison.**

299.— *Charlotte Pierson*, m. ——— Fox.

300.—*Edwin Pierson*, d. young and unm.

301.—*James Pierson.*, m. Miss ——— Howe of Cornwall.

302.—*Adelbert Pierson.*

Children of 224 **Noah Seth Pierson** and **Mary E. Fuller.**

303.—*Nettie Jane Pierson*, b. Feb'y 24, 1865 ; m. Wm. Ostrander.

304.—*Evaline Pierson*, b. July 6, 1869 ; m. Edward Nichols.

305.—*Stephen Curtis Pierson*, b. Aug. 27, 1872 ; unm.

Children of 230 **John Pierson** and **Sarah Lockwood.**

306.—*Frederick Lockwood Pierson*, b. Sept. 23, 1822, at the old
homestead ; all the rest of this family were born at the Stewart
place (now, 1894, occupied by Charles Sabins).

307.—*Mary Elizabeth Pierson*, b. Nov. 19, 1823 ; m. Charles B. Bates of Sharon mountain April 27, 1843, and died in Kent May 25, 1844; buried in Sharon.

308.—*Harriet Louisa Pierson*, b. Feb. 17, 1826 ; m. Henry Kirke White of White Hollow Nov. 26, 1851, and had Josephine, Elizabeth, Albert Pierson and Frances Louisa, all born in Sharon Great Hollow.

309.—*John Albert Pierson*, b. April 6, 1828 ; m. widow Jane Groesbeck (maiden name Jane Briggs) of Saratoga, N.Y., and had one son, Albert Briggs, b. in Torrington, Conn., and drowned there.

310.—*Caroline Pierson*, b. Aug. 7, 1830 ; m. Frederick A. Hotchkiss of Sharon Valley March 27, 1850 ; she died in Bridgeport Dec. 18, 1867, and was buried in Sharon. Their children were *Mary, Carrie, Louisa, Franklin Augustus*, and *Hattie.* Mary married Henry Hill of Reading, Conn.; Frank m. ———— Gillette of Sharon ; Hattie m. ———— McKelvie.

311.—*Sarah Augusta Pierson*, b. Feb. 13, 1833 ; m. Marcus Coon Oct. 26, 1853, and died in Bridgeport Aug. 27, 1866 ; buried in Sharon ; no heirs.

312.—*Frances Aphelia Pierson*, b. Dec. 5, 1834 ; m. Josiah Hawley Mills of North East, N. Y., Nov. 27, 1856. They had one son, who died young, and Emma Cordelia.

313.—*Cordelia Pierson*, b. Nov. 5, 1837 ; unmarried.

314.—*Augustus Pierson*, b. Oct. 31, 1840; d. Aug. 8, 1842.

John Pierson d. in Stanwich Dec. 14, 1888, at 3:30 p. m. ; buried in Stanwich. Sarah Lockwood d. in Stanwich May 21, 1883, in Amenia of typhoid pneumonia; buried in Stanwich. John Pierson was 5 ft. 8 in. high, weight 150 lbs·, hair dark brown, gray eyes, ·nose slightly roman. Sarah Lockwood was above average height, weight 175 lbs., hair dark reddish-brown, blue eyes. The Lockwoods are descended from Robert Lockwood and Susannah St. John, who were in Watertown, Mass., in 1630. Sarah's father was Frederick Lockwood and her mother was Deborah Reynolds, dau, of Nathaniel Reynolds and Sarah Lockwood [*this* Sarah Lockwood was sister of Thaddeus Lockwood]. Frederick Lockwood's father was Jonathan and his mother was Mercy Finch of New Canaan, Conn. Jonathan was son of Still John Lockwood, son of Jonathan, 1st, son of Robert. Jonathan, son of Still John, had Jonathan, Frederick [this Frederick was the author's mother's father], Mary, Mercy, Sarah, Elizabeth, Silas, Amos and Hannah. Mary Ferris, dau. of Geoffrey Ferris of Stamford, was the wife of Jonathan 1st of Greenwich. Robert and Edmund Lockwood, brothers, came over to America in Gov. Winthrop's fleet in 1630.

Children of 232 **Daniel Pierson** and **Electa Ann Reed.**

315.—*George Benjamin Pierson*, b. in Sharon March 27, 1830.

316.—*Julia Ann Pierson*, b. Nov. 27, 1833; she died in Ohio Sept. 13, 1835.

Daniel died in Ellsworth, at the homestead April 13, 1854, of typhoid fever. Electa Ann Reed, who was dau. of Benjamin Reed and Prudence Smith, formerly of Darien, died in Independence, Iowa, Sept. 20th, 1885, and was insane in her last days. Daniel studied law and was admitted to the bar at Litchfield after he was 40 years old. He was a good scholar and had an uncommon good memory. Size 5ft. 8in. high, hair dark brown, eyes black, weight 184 lbs.

Children of 233 **Paulina Pierson** and **Ethan Lord.**

317.—A son, who died young.

318.—*Marietta Lord*, b. in Ellsworth; resides unm. in Gorham, Ontario Co., N. Y. (p. o. Bushville.)

319.—*Flora Louisa Lord*, b. in Ellsworth; m. Frank Foster Feb. 25, 1879, and resides in Gorham.

Ethan Lord d. Feb. 23, 1871, in Gorham; hurt by being thrown from a wagon and died soon after. Paulina Pierson, his wife, died Jan. 3, 1892, in Gorham.

Children of 237 **Almira Pierson** and **Henry St. John.**

320.—*Charles Pierson St. John*, b. Aug. 20, 1839; m. Ella Benson, dau. of Benj. Benson and Chloe Nodine, dau. of John Nodine.

321.—*Aurelia Miles St. John*, b. June 5, 1844; m. William Everett Marsh, son of Elijah Marsh and Lucretia Marvin; no children.

322.—*Cordelia M. St. John*, b. April 8, 1846 ; d. April 4, 1853.

323.—*Pluma Barstow St. John*, b. Dec. 30, 1848 ; m. Horace L. Stannard of Norfolk, Conn. ; no children.

324.—*Isabel St. John*, born Nov. 17, 1859, m. Ebenezer M. Johnson of Cornwall, Conn., and has two children, a daughter (Olive) and a son (Harry).

Children of 243 Eli Pierson, Jr., and Clarissa Tuller.

325.—*Emmeline Pierson*, m. Levi Baldwin ; resides in California.

326.—*Margaret Pierson*, m. ——— Hawley.

327.— *William Eli Pierson*. d. Aug. 29, 1857. in his 21st year.

328.— *George C. Pierson.*

329.—*John L. Pierson.*

330.— *Foster E. Pierson.*

331.—*Sanford W. Pierson.*

332.- -*Charles Pierson.*

333.—*Albert Pierson.*

All the above were born in Egremont, Conn., and all who are living reside in California.   Both Eli Pierson and his wife died in Egremont—he May 4, 1860.

Mrs. Sarah Stillman is authority for saying that the Wakemans and Beers were cousins of the Piersons, through the Clogstones— they being connected.

Children of 247 Lewis Smith Pierson and Elizabeth Boardman,

334.—*George L. Pierson.* m. Mary Hogins of Sheffield ;   resides at Canaan Depot and has two sons.

335.—*Sarah Pierson*, m. Hopkins Candee of Sheffield.

336.—*Levi Pierson*, m. Mary E. Andrews of Northfield, Ct.

337.—*Arthur Pierson*, m. ——— and resides at Ashley Falls.

Children of 129 **Abial Pierson** and **Irene Holbrook**.

338.—*Julius Egbert Pierson*, bap. May 1, 1814, in Derby.

339.—*David Holbrook Pierson*, bap. May 12, 1816, in Derby.

340.—*Melissa Holbrook Pierson*, bap. Aug. 23, 1818, in Derby.

341.—*Irene Pierson*, bap. Oct. 27.———

342.—*Nathan Josiah Pierson*, bap. Sep. 5, 1826, in Derby.

This family removed to Burton, Ohio.

SEVENTH GENERATION.

Children of 264 **William R.Pierson** and **Augusta Wheeler.**
(William R. Pierson was b. Nov. 8, 1818 ; Augusta Wheeler was b.
Nov. 2, 1822.)   This family now reside at Nichols Farms, Conn.

400.—*Mary Augusta Pierson*, b. Sept. 26, 1847 ; m. Sept. 26,
     1866, Lorenzo B. Nichols, who d. Oct. 5, 1876.

401.—*America Pierson* b. Feb. 25, 1850, unmarried.

402.—*Sarah Medora Pierson* b. March 28, 1852, d. Aug. 20, 1854.

Children of 289 **Henry Clark Pierson** and **Charity Slocum.**
They were   married at Pawlings, N. Y., Nov. 4, 1851.   Charity
Slocum was b. in Pawling, May 13, 1823.   Henry C. Pierson d.
in Tonawanda, Erie Co., N. Y., Oct. 27, 1864.

403.—*Emma Pierson* b. at Millville, Orleans Co., N. Y., Dec. 25,
     1852.

404.—*Mary Elizabeth Pierson* b. April 10, 1858, d. May 17, 1859.

405.—*Henry Clark Pierson*, b. in Tonawanda, N.Y., Nov. 7, 1864.

406.—*Emma Pierson*, m. Sept. 14, 1873, R. J. Dean.

Children of 298 **Elizabeth Pierson** and **James H. Bailey.**

407.—*Nettie B. Bailey*, b. March 14, 1860.

408.—*Minnie A. Bailey*, b. July 23, 1862.

409.—*Lillie A. Bailey*, b. April 18, 1865.

410.—*Francis E. Bailey*, b. July 24, 1868.

Children of 309 **Frederick Lockwood Pierson** and **Susan
Skiff.**

They were m. at Ellsworth, Conn., February 2, 1851. Mrs.
Pierson was b. March 2, 1832. Frederick L. Pierson is five feet
eight inches high ; weight, one hundred and sixty pounds; eyes gray
and hair light brown. Mrs. Pierson is five feet four inches ; weight,
one hundred and thirty six pounds ; eyes and hair black.

411.—*Mary Pierson*, b. July 10, 1852, m. Oct. 26, 1875, Joseph

White. She d. May 13, 1888. He d. April 14, 1889. They left a daughter, Clara Louisa White, b. May 28, 1883.

412.—*Edward Pierson*, b. March 3, 1856, m. Jennie Landon. She d. May 22, 1891, without issue.

413.—*Eliza Pierson*, b. April 19, 1860, m. Jan. 2, 1895, Marshall B. Hopkins.

414.— *George Pierson*, b. Oct. 26, 1867, d. unmarried Mar. 1, 1894.

Children of 315 **Dr. George Benjamin Pierson** and **Sophia W. Edgecomb,** his 2nd wife.

He m. first Elizabeth Hatch of Kent, who d. in six months after marriage. He married second Sophia W. Edgecomb, May 26, 1859, at Independence, Iowa. She was b. Dec. 29, 1841. Dr. Geo. B. Pierson studied medicine with Dr. Hatch of Kent, Conn.; practiced awhile in Middlebury, Conn; removed thence to Independence, Iowa, after the death of his father; practiced at Independence for a time, keeping a drug store; enlisted in a Cavalry Regiment during the war, and afterwards removed to Hooper, Nebraska.

415.— *Charles Herbert Pierson*, b. Oct. 16, 1860, in Independence, Iowa.

416.—*Laura Winslow Pierson*, b. Dec. 11, 1864. in Independence, Iowa, m. in Colorado, Oct. 5, 1844, Mr. ——— Layner.

417.—*Henry F. Pierson*, b. Sept. 23, 1866, in Independence, Iowa.

Children of 334 **George L. Pierson** and **Mary Huggins** of Canaan, Conn.

418.— *George Willis Pierson*, b. Nov. 5, 1865.

419.—*Joseph Lewis Pierson*, b. Feb. 8, 1867, m. Clara E. Baldwin.

420.—*Mary Louisa Pierson*, b. May 6, 1869.

421.—*Frederick Smith Pierson*, b. Feb. 26, 1871, m. Eva K. Corbit. Have a son Julius C. Pierson, b. June 30, 1894.

NOTES AND CORRECTIONS.

Page 3, l. 14.—Henry Tomlinson was son of George Tomlinson and Maria Hyde of Yorkshire, England, who was married in Jan., 1600. They removed from Yorkshire to Derby, Derbyshire. Henry was a weaver by trade.

Page 3, l. 21.—The reservoir in Derby is not a town reservoir, but is for the use of the factories in Birmingham.

Page 4, l. 3, etc.—From the old history of Derby it appears that Stephen Pierson had two children, b. before 1670, but their names are not given. A Joseph Pierson drew lots in Derby Mar. 12, 1702, who was probably another son of Stephen.

Page 4, No. 13.—Abigail Pierson m, James St. John, son of James, who was b. March 30, 1738.

Page 5, l. 20.—Abraham Pierson, Sr., was selectman after 1711, and quite frequently until 1741.

Page 8, No. 47.—George M. Pierson studied law with Judge Swan and married his daughter. One of George M.'s children married Prince Von Liner of Prussia.

Page 11, No. 97.—Mr. and Mrs. Tryon removed to New Connecticut, Ohio.

Page 13, No. 126.—Laura Pierson's husband was Moses G. Betts. She was his first wife. His second wife was 250 Caroline Pierson, a niece of the first wife.

Page 13, No. 131.— Hepsey *Peet*, not *Post*.

Page 15, No. 150.--William Pierson bit the animal to preserve his teeth, which it is said never decayed.   He lived to be over 80 years old.

Page 16, No. 184.—Mary *Ann, not* Mary *Allen.*

Page 18, No. 220.—Betsey M. Pierson and Joseph Heath had two children, Abigail Heath b. 1823, and Lewis Heath.

Page 20, Nos. 238, 239, 240, 241.—Strike out.   They were children of 237 Almira Pierson and Henry St. John and appear in their proper place as Nos. 321, 322, 323, and 324 of the sixth generation.

Page 22. No. 124.—Elizabeth Spear was of Bloomfield, N. J., and Moses G. Betts, her son in law, was of Fairfield, Conn.

Page 22 No. 131.—Hepsey *Peet,* not *Post.*

Page 22, No. 265.—Sheldon P. Pierson, Jr., and Lydia J. Hawley were m. Oct. 11, 1855.   His father lived in Trumbull.

Page 23, note to No. 279.—Palmer has since died in states prison.

Page 24, No. 282.—Frank Pierson d. unmarried.   His sister Frances is married.

Page 25, No. 298.—Mrs. Bailey d. in North *Easton* not North *East.*

Page 26, No. 308.—Mr. and Mrs. White's family reside in Winchester.

Page 26, No. 310.—Carrie Louisa (one person) d. about Nov. 1, 1894, unmarried.   Hattie married Sidney McKelvie of Sparta, Ill.

Page 26, No. 314.—Strike out "in Amenia" in 10th line from bottom of page.

Page 27, No. 318.—*Rushville,* not *Bushville.*

Page 28, No. 334.—George L. Pierson's wife was Mary Huggins.   They have three sons and one daughter.

www.ingramcontent.com/pod-product-compliance
Lightning Source LLC
Chambersburg PA
CBHW061239260626
47172CB00003B/933